The Berenstain Bears
and the GREEN-EYED MONSTER

When another bear gets something brand new, the Green-eyed Monster makes <u>you</u> want one, too.

A First Time Book®

The Berenstain Bears
and the GREEN-EYED

Stan & Jan Berenstain

Library of Congress Cataloging-in-Publication Data
Berenstain, Stan The Berenstain Bears and the Green-eyed Monster / by Stan and Jan Berenstain. p. cm. — (First time books) SUMMARY: Sister is overcome with jealousy when Brother gets a shiny new ten-speed bike for his birthday. ISBN: 0-679-86434-2 (pbk.) — 0-679-96434-7 (lib. bdg.)
[1. Bears—Fiction. 2. Jealousy—Fiction. 3. Birthdays—Fiction.]
I. Berenstain, Jan. II. Title. III. Series: Berenstain, Stan. First time books.
PZ7.B4483Beffg 1995 [E]—dc20 93-50109

Manufactured in the United States of America 10 9 8 7 6 5 4 3 2 1

MONSTER

Random House 🏠 New York

It was a happy time in the big tree house down a sunny dirt road in Bear Country—a happy birthday time.

It was Brother Bear's birthday, and he was getting some very fine presents. Brother wasn't exactly having a party, but Cousin Fred, Lizzy Bruin, and Babs Bruno were there. And Gramps and Gran, of course.

"Wow!" said Brother when he opened his present from Gramps. It was an aluminum bat. "Thanks, Gramps. I'll hit twenty home runs with this!"

Gran's present was a great-looking warm-up jacket. Brother tried it on and looked in the mirror. "Thank you, Gran. It's really neat," he said.

His other presents were a fielder's glove from Cousin Fred, a sports video from Lizzy Bruin, and a mystery book from Babs Bruno. Sister's very thoughtful gift was a package of balsa wood, the special wood Brother used for making model airplanes.

"Thank you! Thank you! Thank you all!" he said.
"You're welcome and happy birthday!" said the
gift givers.

Sister's gift *was* thoughtful. But she was being thoughtful in another way, too. It isn't always easy when your brother gets a lot of presents and you don't. Sister understood that she had gotten presents when it was her birthday and would again. Besides, she wasn't that interested in aluminum bats, warm-up jackets, fielder's gloves, sports videos, or balsa wood, anyway.

But all that changed when Mama and Papa Bear gave Brother *their* present. It was the biggest, most beautiful racing bike Sister had ever seen. It had a hand brake, three speeds, and super-sport wheels. When Sister saw that beautiful bike, it was no longer, "Happy birthday, Brother!" It was, "I gotta have that bike! I gotta! I gotta! I gotta!"

Mama saw that I-gotta-have-it look in Sister's eyes. She took her aside and reminded her about all the wonderful presents she had gotten on her last birthday. *But Sister didn't hear a word Mama said.* She just stared at that big, beautiful bike with the hand brake and the super-sport wheels. "Oh, dear," said Mama. "I think you've been taken over by the green-eyed monster."

"Green-eyed monster?" said Sister. "What's that?"

"Oh," said Mama. "That's just a way folks have of talking about jealousy and envy. You know what it means to be jealous. Envy is when you want something that belongs to somebody else."

"But, Mama," said Sister. "It's such a great beautiful bike!"

"Please listen to me, Sister," said Mama. "Even if you had a bike like that, you couldn't ride it. You're not big enough. Your feet wouldn't reach the pedals. Besides, look what Papa's got for you." Papa was wheeling in Brother's junior-size bike with its training wheels attached.

"It's yours now," he said. Sister looked at the bike Brother had outgrown. It was okay, but it didn't have a hand brake, three speeds, and super-sport wheels.

"Come on now," said Mama. "Our guests are leaving. It's time to say good-bye."

"Good-bye!" said Brother. "Thank you all for the wonderful presents!"

"Bye," said Sister. Gramps and Gran got into their pickup truck and headed for home. Lizzy Bruin got into her dad's car with the others. Mr. Bruin had agreed to come for them and drive them home. Then Papa helped carry the new bike down the front steps. Mama and Papa watched proudly as Brother climbed on and tried it out.

First Brother rode big, fast circles
around the tree house. Then he
did a few wheelies. When he started
riding with his feet up on the
handlebars, Mama got worried.
  "Now let's not be
reckless!" she said.

Sister watched, too. She had gone inside and was watching from a window. As she did so she became filled with envy. From the tips of her pink hairbow down to the tips of her toenails, *Sister really wanted that big, beautiful racing bike.*

That night Sister was having trouble falling asleep because she was still thinking about the bike. Then just as her eyes were closing the strangest thing happened. She had a visitor. The visitor looked exactly like Sister, except she was green and had little horns on her head. "I know who you are," Sister said. "You're the green-eyed monster."

Sister was having a dream, of course. But she didn't know that. That's the thing about dreams. They're so *real*.

"Come," said the green-eyed monster. "If you want a bike like Brother's, all you have to do is prove you're big enough to ride it."

Before she quite knew what was happening, she was
up on the bike and the green-eyed monster was giving her
a big push.

The bike was much too big for her. Her feet couldn't even *almost* reach the pedals. Then, as so often happens in dreams, things began to change. The bike got bigger and *bigger* and BIGGER!

Now Sister was speeding down a hill. At the bottom was a great rock. She smashed into it. There was a huge crash! Brother's beautiful new birthday bike flew into a thousand pieces. "What have I done?" she screamed. "What have I done?"

Mama and Papa, who had just fallen asleep, came running into the cubs' room. "Oh, Mama!" cried Sister. "I just smashed Brother's beautiful birthday bike into a thousand pieces! A thousand pieces!"

"Try to calm down, sweetie," said Mama. "Brother's bike is perfectly safe. You were having a dream."

"What's going on?" said Brother, rubbing his eyes.

"I'll go downstairs and get us all some warm milk,"
said Papa. "It'll help us get back to sleep."
    And it did.

The next day Sister's best friend,
Lizzy, came over to play. She and
Sister had a fun time riding around
the yard. Brother's old bike turned
out to be just right for Sister. Lizzy
had a good time on Sister's old trike.
And Brother rode circles around
them on his birthday bike.

Later, when Mr. Bruin came over to pick up Lizzy, he had a very big surprise for everybody. He had just traded in his old car for a beautiful brand-new one. And what a car it was! It had wire wheels, leather seats, and racing stripes.

Mama, Brother, Sister, and Lizzy congratulated
Mr. Bruin on his fine new car. But not Papa. He just
stood and stared. He had the same I-gotta-have-it
look that Sister had when she first saw Brother's
new bike.

"Papa," said Sister. "I think you better watch out for 'you know who'!"

Papa did know who.

"Mr. Bruin," he said, "congratulations on a fine new car!"

After the Bruins drove away,
Mama and Papa sat on the tree
house steps and watched Brother
and Sister do some plain and
fancy bike riding.